DARK WAVES

MIND HACKERS SERIES: NOVELLA

AMANDA UHL

Published in the United States by Amanda Uhl, LLC.

Dark Waves. Copyright © 2022 by Amanda Uhl
www.amandauhl.com

Print ISBN: 978-1-952581-05-2
Digital ISBN: 978-1-952581-04-5

Cover by Christian Betulan
www.coversbychristian.com

To my son, Sam, and to my critique partners, Cathy Matuszak and Joyce Caylor. Thank you for sharing your superpower plotting skills with me. I couldn't have written this story without you.

CHAPTER ONE

Keeping secrets wasn't easy when your patient could hack into your mind. Audrey Gilbert adjusted her reading glasses and gave the gentleman reclining in her office chair a stern look. "Jake Hall, must I remind you you're the patient, and I'm the psychiatrist? I'm glad you're feeling better, but let's use our last session to focus on your future rather than my current situation, shall we?"

Jake stretched his hands behind his head. "It doesn't take a mind hacker to know when you're worried, Doc. The least I can do is offer a listening ear. Because of you, I'll be returning to my old team in the CMU at the end of the month."

Up until a year ago, Jake had been a member of the Cognitive Mind Unit, or CMU, an elite group of psychics. Jake was trained to hack into minds and could erase and change thoughts. But like most young recruits new to the job, he began exhibiting signs of burnout six months ago and was sent to the Corvey Institute in Chicago for evaluation.

Audrey managed a professional smile. "While I appreciate the offer, it's not something I can share with you. Physician-patient privilege and all."

"For the record, I wasn't trying to hack into your mind. You were projecting."

Audrey sighed and pressed two fingers against the pain in her temple—another headache was starting. Hackers were sensitive to emotion, which had always been a struggle for her in treating them. Where there was strong emotion, there was energy. And energy fueled their paranormal powers. She took a deep breath and let it out slowly. "Sorry about that."

Her cell phone buzzed, catching her by surprise since she'd set it to only ring if… She scrambled to search her pockets.

"Excuse me. I need to take this call. I'll be right back."

She stepped into the hallway, heart pumping, grateful the doors were soundproof in the high-tech facility.

"Hello, Rich. You have an update?"

Rich Conpath was her new boss at the Corvey Institute and not the friendliest of sorts, even on a good day. Early this morning, a former patient had brought a rifle to a local liquor store and shot up the place. Only the store owner had been inside at the time.

"Where are you?"

Audrey's stomach sank. "I'm standing in the hallway outside my office."

"Alone?"

"Yes, there's no one with me. Did the store owner survive?"

There was a long pause on the other end. "No, he did not."

"Oh my God." Audrey's stomach sank even further, and the pain in her head intensified. An innocent man had been killed. A man who had a family…maybe a wife and children. She leaned against the wall so her legs didn't collapse from under her, and closed her eyes. "How horrible. Did Luke hurt anyone else?"

"No, the hacker's in police custody."

She opened her eyes and took a breath. "Thank God."

"There's going to be an investigation, of course. Your methods are unusual, to say the least."

"I…I understand. But… My God…I can't believe it. It makes no sense he would go rogue. I did nothing I haven't done with all my patients. He had made a complete recovery."

"Apparently not, and you *were* the one to sign his release. There will be repercussions."

"Re…repercussions? What do you mean?"

There was a short pause, and Audrey braced for the worst.

"I was going to wait to tell you when I could see you in person, but I won't be back in Chicago for another week. I'm afraid I'm going to have to relieve you from your duties until further notice."

Audrey gasped and clutched the phone to her ear. "You're firing me?"

"You made a grave error in judgment when you released the patient from your care. The CMU cannot afford errors of this magnitude. You knew the risks when you took the job. You're contractually responsible for his actions."

She swallowed the sudden dryness in her throat. The risk of a hacker going rogue was always a potential threat, since they frequently suffered from emotional, physical, and mental exhaustion caused by excessive and prolonged stress on the job.

"Yes, but, up until now, I've had a perfect track record. Look, I feel awful about this, and I agree it looks bad for the CMU, but I assure you the patient in question passed all the usual tests, or I never would have signed his release. Doesn't that count for anything?"

Rich cleared his throat. "As a matter of fact, it does. I've been instructed to offer you a deal. There *is* a way you can earn your job back if you're interested."

"Deal? How?" She suspected the anxiousness came across in her voice, although she tried to control the panic coursing through her system. If she didn't have her job, she couldn't pay her bills, and if she couldn't pay her bills, she couldn't continue to pay for her mother's around-the-clock care. She swiped a sweaty palm against her pants.

"Another job. It will involve an extended stay in Ohio—Marblehead, to be exact."

"Marblehead? Is that a suburb in Cleveland?"

"Not exactly. It's a remote town on Lake Erie near Sandusky."

"Why there?"

"Marblehead happens to be the home of a former mind hacker, Kevin Jorgensen. The CMU wants him back on the job, but he refuses to cooperate. Nearly lost his life a few years back and suffers from post traumatic stress syndrome—among other things."

Rich didn't describe the other things, but Audrey had some ideas. Ex-hackers could experience any number of symptoms, from trouble concentrating to irrational thoughts to hallucinations.

She ran her fingers through her hair. Over the years, she'd seen and treated numerous mental health ailments. That's why it was so surprising her patient had gone rogue. Not after she'd spent so much time with him and had seen such dramatic improvement. "You're saying all I have to do is convince one person to return to work, and I can get my job back?"

"That's correct. But it won't be easy."

"Why?"

"Jorgensen is a recluse and unstable. He lives alone and doesn't socialize. He'll resent your intrusion on his solitude."

"Sounds like my typical patient."

There was another short pause, and Audrey shifted from one foot to the other. "What aren't you telling me?"

"Er…he's not your *typical* patient."

"He has a physical disability? He's deaf or blind or something?"

"No, his physical health is top-notch."

"Then what is it?"

"He's a powerhouse talent—class ten on the psychic scale. If he would take a dislike to you, he could do some serious damage to your mind…maybe erase your memories, cause permanent brain damage, or even death."

Goose bumps moved up her arms. Her mouth was open, and she clamped it shut. "Well above my pay level then. Why would the CMU think I could help him?"

"That's the million-dollar question. I don't know the answer. His brother, Jordan, is also a class ten, but

Kevin refuses to have anything to do with him or the rest of his family. Maybe the CMU thinks you'll have more success. The only thing I know for certain is, if you can turn Kevin Jorgensen around, you can return to the office. Will you do it?"

Audrey thought of her dwindling bank account and her mother's ongoing care, not to mention her sister's tuition due at the end of the month. Jobs for paranormal psychiatrists outside the CMU were scarce. She'd be unlikely to find another any time soon. And although she could never bring the innocent liquor store owner back to life, if she could rehabilitate Jorgensen, it would help assuage her guilt.

"I don't think I have much of a choice."

CHAPTER TWO

Kevin Jorgensen gritted his teeth, hunched his shoulders, and headed into the only grocery store in the small town he called home. He made the trip once a month out of necessity, and every time he did, he wondered if today would be the day.

The day he finally lost his mind and killed someone.

He entered the packed building, dodging a mother pushing her cart with a toddler sitting in the front, legs dangling. Did it look more crowded this morning? He checked his watch. *Damn.* It was a Saturday—no wonder there were so many people and lots of kids. Living alone often made him forget the day of the week.

He didn't pause, but grabbed a cart and moved forward, making his way to the produce section and onto the bakery, where he nabbed a loaf of bread. He had entered the canned soup aisle and was reaching for some chicken noodle soup when he heard his name.

He was pretty certain the voice was in his mind and not coming from someone's mouth.

He almost dropped the soup can but managed to throw it into his cart and glance around at the shoppers nearby. No one knew him here. He kept a low profile. Was he hallucinating? He didn't have the disturbing sense of unreality he normally felt with a hallucination.

Behind him, an older woman considered a box of crackers before putting it back on the shelf. From the puzzled look on her face, he guessed she was real—his delusions were usually a bit more menacing. His gaze moved on to a young couple arguing over the canned vegetables while their kids raced up and down the aisle. The voice had been a woman's voice, and he didn't think it had come from either of them. That left…?

Frowning, he pushed his cart around the corner to the other side of the aisle. A slim young woman was hunched over her cell phone in front of the salad dressing. She had pale skin that looked like it hadn't seen the sun in some time and black, glossy hair that shone under the fluorescent lights. She wore faded jeans and a green army jacket that somehow suited her.

He pretended to be looking for dressing, too, while he probed her thoughts. Without a partner—a trainer who could magnify energy waves—it was impossible to fully hack into the woman's mind. But he was strong enough to catch stray thoughts now and then, and the lady was obviously feeling emotional, because he heard quite a few.

$8.99 way too much…summer tuition due soon…why I need…wasn't my fault…how hard can it be…Kevin Jorgensen.

There it was again. It wasn't his brain dreaming up something that wasn't there. This lady in front of him was real.

And she knows my name.

The hair on the back of his neck rose, and his gut clenched almost painfully. How did a stranger know his name, and what the hell was she doing in Marblehead in *his* grocery store? The coincidence—if it was a coincidence—was incredible.

The woman put the dressing back on the shelf and continued making her way down the aisle. He followed behind, using every bit of talent he possessed to continue to hear what she was thinking.

…eat tuna tonight…do research…have to find him in the morning…

Shit. She couldn't be thinking about tracking him down, could she?

…lives like a hermit…won't like me…doesn't like strangers…

She grabbed a box of spaghetti and a jar of sauce before making her way to the cash register. All the while, Kevin was careful to keep his distance, all six senses on high alert as he watched her move through the check out.

Who was she, and what did she want with him?

The woman turned slightly as she headed to the exit, and he caught her side profile—a sharp nose and angular chin, which hinted at a stubborn determination, and a long curve to her neck.

Something powerful raced through him, sending a tingle down his spine, and he stepped forward. The woman shifted, turned in his direction, and their eyes caught for a moment before she looked away. Even at a distance he could see her irises were a clear, soft gray, like the mist above a hot sidewalk after an unexpected summer rain. A thrill of excitement rippled through his veins.

She pushed her cart out the door, and he realized he was still staring at the exit like a dimwit, and hadn't put more than a loaf of bread and a can of soup in his cart.

CHAPTER THREE

Audrey carried the groceries up the steps and into the one-room efficiency she'd decided on due to its low monthly rent and its proximity to downtown Marblehead. The apartment was situated over a popular beach boutique, which sold clothing and accessories and was gearing up for the summer season. The sound of James Taylor crooning about Carolina could be heard through the cracks in the wood floor.

She paused to study the empty room and consider her next steps. First, she had to put the food away, and second, she had to consider what she could purchase to brighten up the place. Maybe some flowers and books?

Of course, improving her surroundings would not help get her job back. She put the groceries away, moving back and forth from the single table where she'd set the bags to the fridge and cupboards. She needed to study Kevin Jorgensen's dossier and make plans for tomorrow.

She finished with the groceries and made herself a cup of tea, which she heated in the small microwave. Then she sat in one of two chairs at the kitchen table and studied the open folder in front of her. A glossy headshot of Jorgensen stared back at her.

She squinted at the photo, which looked familiar, but she knew she had never been introduced to Kevin. She would have remembered him. He had wheat-colored hair, wide blue eyes, and an almost sweet expression on his face. He couldn't have been much above twenty-five in the photo, but it was taken some time ago. He was probably closer to thirty by now.

She turned to the paperwork and read over the other basic details.

Height: 6'4"
Weight: 180 lbs.
Ethnicity: Norwegian and English
Birthplace: Kansas City, Missouri
Marital Status: Single
Talent: Telepathic
Class: 10

A single word jumped out at her from the bottom of the page where there was some additional background information. *Psychotic.*

A familiar tremor ran through her veins, and her heart lurched.

"What happened to the sweet young boy you were, Kevin Jorgensen?" She bit her lip.

This was how it always began—with a question. A nagging question that had her running down a rabbit hole looking for answers. Each question led to the next and the next, until, eventually, she arrived at a solution.

She took a sip of tea and continued reading the notes, paying close attention to every detail. It was the details that would provide the answer when the time came. When she had finished reading, her tea was cold and she knew two things: What had happened to Kevin was so traumatic it had altered his personality, and this job would be her most difficult yet.

She set the notes aside and studied the address. How should she approach the patient? Should she ring his doorbell and hope he'd answer? If he did, he wouldn't welcome her with open arms. From the report she'd read, the man was a loner and unpredictable. Audrey didn't want to be on the other end of his psychic whammy.

She got up from the table and washed her teacup. No, the direct approach wouldn't work well with a man like Jorgensen. There was nothing for it, she'd have to stake out his place and observe him for a while. Maybe she could befriend him as a casual acquaintance. If he didn't know Audrey was sent to rehabilitate him, he might be willing to confide in her as a friend.

She finished cleaning just as her cell phone buzzed—Chelsea, her sister.

"Hello, Chels. Everything okay?"

"Everything's fine. I got your message that you're temporarily moving to Ohio."

"That's right."

"What about Mom?"

"Mom will be fine. She's receiving great care at the nursing home. And I'll still call her every day like I do now."

"How long are you going to be in Ohio?"

"I'm not sure. Only a couple of months, hopefully. How's school?" she asked, more to redirect the conversation. She'd rather not have to tell Chelsea she'd lost her job. Her sister was a second year straight-A Harvard student in a challenging medical program. She didn't need any distractions.

"Fine. I think I'm going to like my classes this semester."

"Great."

"I've kinda… Well, I met someone."

The words were so unexpected, Audrey felt like she'd been doused with a bucket of cold water. "Who…how?"

Her sister laughed, clearly relishing Audrey's surprise. "I know I said I'm never getting married, and that's still kind of true, but…his name is Cory and he wants to travel the world and he loves the outdoors like I do and he says he's never met someone like me before and—"

"Where did you meet Cory?" Audrey interrupted, understanding it was the fastest way to get the essential details.

"Online. He's part of a group I play games with every week. He can't play worth shit, but he's funny and everyone likes him."

"It's an online relationship then?"

"It *was* an online relationship, but we met last week in person and again yesterday. He's commuting this semester, so I can only see him the days he's on campus."

"It sounds like you're getting serious fast."

"That's why I'm telling you about him. I didn't think I'd ever feel this way about someone else…you know…after witnessing Mom and Dad's crappy relationship. But Cory is not like a lot of the immature guys around here. He's got plans and goals. He wants to be a computer engineer."

"How old is he?"

"Twenty-eight. He took a few years off from school before getting his act together. He says he knows what he wants now and is willing to work hard for it."

Audrey cringed—the guy was eight years older than Chelsea, which was closer to Audrey's age. Why would a twenty-eight-year-old be going after a twenty-year-old?

She swallowed her fear along with the saliva in her mouth. Chelsea was no longer a little girl, she reminded herself. It wasn't fair to smother her sister to the point she couldn't make up her own mind about who to date.

She took a breath and deliberately lowered her voice. "Cory sounds wonderful, and I'm glad you're telling me, but I wouldn't be any kind of older sister if I didn't caution you about taking things slow and focusing on your schoolwork. You're smart, but you can't afford distractions if you want to keep your scholarship."

"I know. And I know how hard you're working to help me pay for school. I won't stop studying, I promise."

"Of course, you won't," Audrey said. "I'm just being a paranoid older sister. But be cautious, okay? You're all I've got."

"I know…I will. Love ya, sis."

"Love you, too. Listen, it's late, and I have to get an early start tomorrow on my latest assignment. I'll give you a call later in the week."

They disconnected, and Audrey studied the cell phone in her hand. Something about the call had her on edge. Life was changing faster than she wanted it to. One day her sister would no longer need Audrey. She'd marry someone and live far away, and all Audrey would have would be her job—if she still had a job—and a mother who barely recognized her.

She set the phone down and moved to turn the light out, a deep emptiness filling her heart.

One day soon, she'd be even more alone than she was now.

CHAPTER FOUR

Kevin threw the empty can of beer toward the wastebasket in the kitchen and missed. It bounced on the hard tile with a metallic clang and landed next to a pile of empties. He reached for another, cracked it open, and took a sip. Maybe if he drank himself into oblivion, he wouldn't see the terrifying hallucination in front of him.

The dark shadow took shape, blotting out the light from the kitchen. A woman shook her finger at him. *"You are a disgrace to humankind."*

He pretended not to hear the old hag. Despite her authoritative voice, she looked tiny and was dressed in some sort of long skirt that went almost to her ankles. Her dark hair was tied into a knot on the top of her head. Maybe if he didn't look at her, she'd disappear. He took another sip of beer and pretended to watch the local news on the television.

"No one will ever love you. Not when you don't take care of yourself."

The phantom lady was standing in front of him now, giving him a cutting stare. It was impossible not to look at her.

She glared at him. *"Aren't you going to answer me?"*

He groaned inwardly and took another long swig of his beer. "You're not real, Hilda." That was his name for the vision, since she'd never confessed hers.

"Are you going to lay around all day? What a loser you've turned out to be."

"Go away, Hilda."

She tipped her head back and laughed. The sound was so horrible it sent a shiver down Kevin's spine. He jumped up and went to the fridge, looking for something to distract him, chanting under his breath, "There's no one there, there's no one there, there's no one there."

Hilda continued laughing, and the sound seemed to reverberate through the small space.

Kevin pressed his fists against his ears. He couldn't stand it any longer; he had to get out of the house. He stumbled to the door, yanked it open, and headed to the porch.

The old woman followed, taunting, *"Lazy, good-for-nothing son-of-a-bitch."*

His stomach rumbled a warning, and Kevin knew he was going to be sick. He headed down the steps, nearly tripping over his own feet in his haste to get away. He stood over the bushes and willed his stomach to stay strong, but it didn't listen. He wasn't sure how long he remained there, hunched over, gagging—long enough for his imaginary witch to leave him, but not without one last jibe.

"You're disgusting," she whispered in his ear.

She wasn't wrong.

Hilda was one of two distinct hallucinations Kevin experienced. The other was Abe—a tall, gaunt figure who liked to wake him up in the middle of the night but was blessedly silent the rest of the time.

Thank God.

He dropped to his knees and pressed his nose to the ground, breathing in the reassuring smell of fresh grass.

"Here, take this," a woman said.

At first, he thought she was another hallucination, but as he squinted up at the female standing over him, thrusting a water bottle into his face, he knew better. The imaginary people who visited him daily didn't wear sympathetic smiles, and he recognized this woman. She had haunted him ever since their encounter last week in the supermarket.

He forced air into his starved lungs. He'd known he'd see her again sooner or later—except he'd hoped it'd be later. And not in the midst of this horrible retching. His stomach rumbled, and he pressed his lips together.

"Who are you?"

"I'm Audrey Gilbert. Drink some water. You'll feel better."

She was prettier than he'd first thought, a smattering of freckles over pale cheeks, wide, gray eyes, and full lips. She smelled of lavender, and it didn't make him want to gag. Like the grass, he wanted only to breathe her in. He fought an unexpected urge to touch her skin to see if it was as soft as it looked.

"Go on." She shook the water bottle at him. "Drink."

He took the offering and stood, towering over her—she couldn't be much above five feet—and cracked the lid.

"Why are you here?" The urge to vomit faded, his psychic senses on full alert.

"I was walking by and happened to see you…er…losing your lunch. You looked like you could use some help."

She lied. He caught the echo of her thoughts, and he recognized her from their encounter in the store. He didn't need to read her mind to know this was no casual meet-and-greet. The woman had stalked him. But why?

"Thank you for the water."

He turned and headed toward the house. Her explanation didn't matter. And that he found her attractive didn't matter. He lived alone in this remote town for a good reason. And he aimed to keep it that way.

"Wait…please."

Why was he pausing? He should keep moving, but he found himself stopping and turning around.

"What?"

"I'd like to talk to you."

"Okay, talk."

She blinked but didn't turn away at his brusque tone. "Can we sit on the porch?"

He didn't bother answering, but moved forward, and she followed close behind as he knew she would. Whatever Audrey Gilbert wanted, she wouldn't let his rude behavior hinder her efforts. And he was just curious enough to listen.

He motioned to a chair on the porch, and he found a spot opposite on the swing. He set it in motion with one foot, took another swig of water, and waited for her to speak.

"I can help you manage your illness."

He laughed, although he wasn't amused. "You mean what you just witnessed? That's what happens when you drink too much." *And you receive a visit from Hilda.*

"No, I mean I can help you with your other symptoms."

Psychotic episodes. Her thought seemed to jump out and punch him in the face. Now she *did* have his attention, and he stilled the forward motion of the swing.

"Who are you?"

"I told you. My name is Audrey Gilbert."

"Please tell me you're not a shrink." But that's exactly what she was—he could read the truth in her mind. After the accident, he'd gone back to work until the visitations started. He'd seen at least a dozen shrinks. All of them said he suffered from a severe psychotic disorder, triggered by the trauma he'd experienced when he'd been ejected prematurely from a target's mind. Part of his mind had been wiped, and he'd lost touch with reality, which explained Hilda and Abe and the other shadowy figures he sometimes saw and heard.

He took another sip of water. Several of the shrinks had put him on antipsychotic drugs, some had tried meditation and hypnotism, a few had ordered him hospitalized. Before they could try any more experimental treatments, he'd quit the CMU and the shrinks and escaped to Marblehead, where he enjoyed his drug of choice—beer. That was five years ago.

"I prefer the term 'paranormal psychiatrist' myself."

Kevin shrugged. A shrink was a shrink in his view. But Audrey Gilbert had not raised her voice or gotten defensive. He liked that about her. There was something calming about her presence. Soothing, like the glass of warm milk his mom used to make him after a paranormal nightmare when he was a child.

"I specialize in healing hackers who suffer from post-traumatic stress syndrome. I'd like to help you. Will you give me the chance?"

He should tell her to get lost, but he found he was reluctant to let her go. Curiosity? Or maybe a touch of loneliness. It had been weeks since his last conversation with a real person.

"What makes you think your treatment will work?"

"I have a near perfect track record with my patients." *Until today.*

Did she know how much she was projecting? He hadn't even had to work to pluck the thought from her brain. "What happened today?"

Her startled gaze met his, and he tried hard not to smile at her confusion.

"You're reading my mind?"

"Not deliberately." Although he wouldn't hesitate to use his talent if needed. Something about his new shrink made him want to know her better.

Much, much better.

Get your mind out of the gutter, Jorgensen.

She sighed. "A former patient went rogue and killed someone."

"And you're to blame?"

"Not directly, but…yes. I made the decision to allow him to re-enter society. I signed the papers to have him released."

"Why are you here then? Shouldn't you be home—wherever that is—cleaning up the mess you made?"

"I…" *I've been fired.*

She hesitated, pink staining her smooth cheeks. How was it a CMU shrink had no mental blocks in place? It would be easy for a talent far less powerful to read her mind. He didn't even have to try.

"I've been asked to look into your case. Despite my recent screw-up, I've had some success rehabilitating hackers with similar issues to yours. I think I can help you."

"How?"

A cool wind blew off the lake, and she wrapped her arms around herself. She had nice hands—long, tapered fingers, and the tips of her nails were painted a pale pink.

"Talking about the trauma you experienced generally helps. There are also techniques I can teach you that can make it easier to handle your symptoms."

"What kind of techniques?"

"Basic stuff—like forming good habits to help you manage your stress, eat healthy, exercise, and get a proper amount of sleep."

"You're going to teach me how to take care of myself."

"Yes, if you'll let me." Behind Audrey, a dark shadow took shape, and he almost groaned out loud. *Why now?*

"What is it?" Audrey asked.

Hilda shook her head and wagged a finger. *"You're gonna screw this up, ya bonehead."*

He ignored the phantom and focused on Audrey. What had they been talking about? Oh, yes, healthy habits.

Hilda moved in front, blocking his view, and glared. *"You will end up alone, you sick bastard."*

"Kevin, what's wrong? Are you okay?"

"If you won't seek help, why don't you do the world a favor and put an end to your miserable existence."

"No…" He rubbed his eyes, trying to squeeze Hilda out of sight, but it didn't work. The crone stood in front of him, cackling, her eyes boring holes into his soul. He was so damn tired of fighting for his sanity.

Maybe Hilda was right. Maybe the world would be better off without him.

He shuddered and dropped his head into his hands.

Strong arms gripped his shoulders, shaking him. Hilda laughed, and the sound scraped across sensitive eardrums. Maybe he'd finally lost it? Hilda had never grabbed him before. Bile rose in his throat, suffocating him, and his whole body stiffened with the effort it took to remain on the swing.

Hilda squeezed harder. "You'll be okay, Kevin. I promise."

He opened his eyes, half expecting to see the old hag in front of him, but it was the shrink, Audrey, gazing at him with sympathy. "Let's get you in the house," she said.

CHAPTER FIVE

Audrey half held, half dragged Kevin into his house and managed to get him onto the couch, where he groaned and collapsed into the pillows. She crouched beside him and unlaced his tennis shoes.

"What are you doing?" He didn't move.

"Taking your shoes off so you can lay down and get some rest."

"I don't need to sleep. I just need a minute."

"Either way, you'll do better with your shoes off."

Kevin snorted his exasperation, but Audrey ignored him, pulling off one shoe and the other before moving away. "How long have you been experiencing these episodes?" She kept her tone matter of fact and waited. Sometimes patients wanted to talk; sometimes they didn't. A lot depended on their mental state and how well they trusted the person asking—and she wanted him to trust her.

Kevin sighed. "How long have you been a shrink?"

Sometimes, the more challenging patients asked the questions.

"Five years."

He still hadn't moved from his position, but Audrey felt the laser-sharp attention he directed her way in her bones. Was he reading her mind? A class ten talent could also manipulate her thoughts if he wanted.

She shivered and stood a little taller, crossing her arms. Maybe walking up to Kevin as he was upchucking in the bushes wasn't one of her more brilliant ideas. But she hadn't been able to think of another way to approach him, and it seemed like the perfect opportunity both personally and professionally.

"Why are you hovering over me and shaking like a leaf?" He squinted at her, a knowing expression on his face. "If you're not going to psychoanalyze me, which I wouldn't advise at the moment, why don't you make yourself useful and get us both a cup of coffee? The pot's on the counter."

More to get out from under his hard gaze than to play servant, Audrey headed into the kitchen.

"Mugs are in the cupboard to the right of the stove." His deep voice followed her.

She found two brown ceramic mugs and filled them with the blackest coffee she'd seen in some time. Now, where would he hide the cream and sugar?

"I'm not much for cream, but there's milk in the fridge and sugar in the cupboard over the microwave."

He *was* reading her mind. Audrey swallowed and mentally berated herself. She'd need to tamp down her emotions if she didn't want him knowing her every thought.

She busied herself locating the milk and sugar, reminding herself to breathe. She added a teaspoon of sugar to his mug and doubled it in her own, adding as much milk as she could fit. She carried both mugs into the dining room and handed him one, keeping her thoughts blank.

He sat up and took it, gesturing at a recliner nearby. "Sorry, my manners are a little rusty. Make yourself comfortable."

She removed a stack of dusty magazines from the chair and sat.

"I'm not much used to visitors," he said, his tone dry. Was it her imagination, or were his cheeks a little red?

"It's okay." She took a sip of coffee and tried hard not to grimace at the bitter taste. Silence stretched between them, broken only by the sound of a motorcycle passing along the road out front. She set the coffee down on a side table beside her chair and searched for a neutral topic. "How long have you lived in Marblehead?"

"You already know the answer."

Her heart skipped a beat, and her gaze flew to his, tension racing along her nerve endings. If he'd wanted to provoke her, he'd succeeded.

"Why do you keep reading my mind? I don't recall inviting you to the party."

She *did* know how long he'd been in the town. That information had been in the report she'd scoured over the last week. What she didn't know was what the little episode on the porch had been about and why he'd chosen to live alone in this remote place, far away from his family and friends. The file said he had parents living, plus his brother, Jordan. Why had Kevin turned his back on everyone he held dear?

He moved forward, and she flinched, half expecting him to rise from the chair and strike her. But he set his cup on the coffee table in front him and smiled, which had the effect of making him look years younger and almost handsome underneath the scruff. "One thing you ought to know about me. I'll never need an invitation to the party when you leave the door wide open."

She glared at him, but he held up a hand. "If you work with psychics, then you must understand. We can't help but read a person's thoughts when they're projecting. It's like asking us to not notice when someone sets off the fire alarm."

He was right, of course. There was no use getting upset with him. The stress of her job must be taking a toll. Lately, she'd seemed to become an open book for every hacker out there to read—even lower-class talents. She dropped her gaze to her fingers, which she had clenched in her lap, and unfolded them one by one.

"All righty then, let me ask you something I don't know." She raised her head until their gazes locked. "What happened out there on the porch earlier?"

He curled his lip like a tiger with a sore paw, and his voice sounded weary and bitter. "You know the answer to that question, too."

Psychotic episodes.

The ominous words were a dark cloud hanging between them. They were just words on a page, really. They didn't explain what Kevin had experienced. She needed to hear him describe what happened in his own words. Needed to get to the underlying emotions. To understand his pain. Only then could he begin to heal.

"Do you want to tell me about it?"

"Not particularly. What happened to your father?"

The words settled in her lungs like a shard of ice, making it hard to snatch a breath. "You… What…" How the hell had he learned about her father? She rarely thought about the man these days.

"Tsk, tsk. Not true," Kevin shook his head at her and set his empty coffee mug next to him on the couch, meeting the shocked surprise on her face with a bland look. "You think about him more often than you'd like. What were his last words to you?" He frowned, considering. "Something like, 'Take care of your mother, kid.'"

Hot tears rushed to her eyes, and she blinked, hoping he didn't notice. "You have no right to invade my private thoughts."

"It's not good to suppress your feelings, Doc. All that pent-up emotion is fuel for someone like me."

He got up from the couch and moved toward her, and she was reminded again of his unpredictable nature and the fact they were alone together. Her stomach quivered. What had she been thinking? Confronting him in his home was a bad, bad idea.

He leaned over the chair, causing her heart to beat hard, but he only collected her mug from the table. His warm breath caressed her cheeks as he straightened.

"I can't help what I am, Doc. Remember that."

He turned and went into the kitchen, leaving Audrey feeling like she'd been zapped with an invisible stun gun. Kevin Jorgensen was armed and dangerous, and he wanted her to know it. This was a warning, pure and simple: keep out of his business, or he would mess with hers. And tapping into a suppressed memory was probably only a tenth of the damage he could cause. She was out of her element.

Audrey was a lot of things, but she wasn't stupid.

She got up, collected her purse and car keys, and made her way to the front door, hardly knowing what she was doing. She reached for the knob before she reconsidered. She couldn't give up on this assignment. Too many people were counting on her. Besides, she hadn't survived an awful childhood by quitting, and something inside her refused to give up on Kevin.

She turned and flashed him a bright smile. "See you tomorrow. I'll bring the coffee."

She had the satisfaction of witnessing the surprise on his face before she slammed the door behind her.

Kevin didn't flinch as the door closed behind the stubborn shrink, but he didn't move from his spot in the kitchen, either. He wasn't proud of the methods he'd employed on the good doctor, but it seemed like the only way of getting her to leave him in peace.

So why did he feel an insane desire to run after her, apologize, and beg her to come back?

He shuffled into the dining room, his gaze settling on the armchair where she had sat, poised like a pale little bird ready to take flight. She feared him, that much he knew, and she was right to fear him. There was a good reason he kept himself far away from those he loved. Even he didn't know the damage he was capable of inflicting.

He sighed and walked to the window, wishing he'd thought to look for her car earlier. No vehicles were parked on the street out front. She said she'd return tomorrow, and he couldn't contain the leap of excitement in his veins at the thought. He had warned her, and she'd chosen to ignore the warning. He couldn't be responsible for what might happen between them.

He plucked the paperback, *The Secret to Meditation*, he'd been reading from the stack of books on the floor and sat on the couch. But after ten minutes of reading the same passage over and over, he set the book aside. There was no use hiding from the truth: Audrey's visit had stirred his senses in a way he hadn't experienced in a good long while. And he liked the sensation a whole hell of a lot.

When he'd punctured her thoughts, he had been purposeful in his search, going after a singular suppressed memory rather than a total invasion of her privacy. It had been surprisingly easy without a trainer to unearth the memory—a child of seventeen or eighteen watching her father walk away, leaving her alone with a boozehound mother and a younger sister of five. He'd tasted her fear and rage as her father had left the house forever. He'd felt her tears. He was awed by her courage.

He made his way to the kitchen, digging in the cupboard where he kept a single metal pot, and filled it with water. Something nagged at him, some detail he had missed.

He put the pot on the stove, covered it with the lid, and waited. It was true what they said about a watched pot—it seemed endless before the first bubbles rose to the surface. He had lifted the lid and added the pasta when a dark face formed in the steam.

"If you are careless, she will die," Abe moaned.

Kevin grunted and dropped the lid, which clanged and skidded on the floor until it hit the cabinet door.

Abe only visited in the dead of night, and he never spoke. Yet here he was in the early evening with a dire warning.

"You don't remember?" Abe moaned in his ear.

Remember? What was there to remember? Kevin stepped away. He didn't like to look at the soulless eyes of his uninvited guest for fear he'd become a lunatic.

Kevin's brain had been wiped during the accident—some of his memories stolen. And now he had to listen to this phantom berating him for not remembering what was impossible to recover. He gritted his teeth and retrieved the lid, setting it on the counter and turning the burning down to low.

The fully formed figure now stood beside Kevin and pointed a shadowy finger into his face. *"You must remember—her life depends on it."*

Her life? Did Abe mean Audrey? Usually, the apparitions either whispered or scolded him. They never referred to others. What was so special about Audrey?

The flash of insight came so quickly, he stilled, hardly daring to breath.

There had been a white patch in Audrey Gilbert's mind.

He mulled that fact over while he paced back and forth between the kitchen and dining room. It had been a few years since he'd deliberately hacked into someone's mind without a trainer, so he hadn't paid enough attention to the small spot of white—a missing memory.

His head throbbed and he clutched his skull, praying he didn't end up with a migraine. Audrey Gilbert's mind had been wiped. There was no doubt about it. What was worse, he thought he recognized the paranormal signature of the hacker.

CHAPTER SIX

Kevin was waiting at the window when Audrey pulled into the drive at noon. She caught the flash of white curtain before it settled in place.

She expected to have to ring the doorbell multiple times to get him to answer, but she was wrong. No sooner had she reached the porch steps when the door opened and all six feet four of manly muscle filled the opening. Her heart leaped.

"Where have you been?"

"Wh…What?" He wanted to see her?

"It's lunchtime. You said you would bring the coffee," he grumbled.

"I did bring the coffee." She held up the thermos she carried, along with her notebook and pen.

He grimaced and rolled his eyes but stepped aside so she could enter. "Who brings coffee to lunch? I expected you for breakfast."

"I do." Audrey couldn't help but smile at the sincere annoyance in his voice. Despite his surliness, he didn't look as scruffy as the previous day. He appeared to have showered and shaved and had run a comb through his golden hair. She now noticed what she had tried to avoid acknowledging yesterday.

Kevin Jorgensen was a handsome and virile man, and something deep inside her responded.

She made her way to the kitchen and proceeded to find the same two mugs in the cupboard from yesterday and fill them with the hot brew. He followed, hovering far too close, the fresh scent of the soap he used hanging in the air.

"Go ahead, taste it," she said, offering him the mug after she'd added a teaspoon of sugar. "I'll think you'll notice a big improvement over the black tar we had yesterday."

He took a sip, his brilliant blue eyes meeting hers.

"Well?" she asked when he didn't say anything.

He shrugged. "It's decent."

She turned away from his grudging admission to hide her smile, grabbed her notebook, and made her way to the recliner where she'd sat yesterday.

"Good, I'll take that as progress. Now, let's talk about how I can help you."

"You can start by putting down the notebook, Doc."

She hesitated but complied. If setting aside her notebook got him to talk, so be it. She'd have to rely on her memory, which was normally excellent.

He made his way to the couch and sat, stretching his long legs in front of him.

"Okay then." She entwined her fingers together on her lap and lowered her gaze, doing her best to look safe. "How about you tell me how you're feeling today?"

He laughed but it sounded bitter. "Hung over."

"How often do you drink alcohol?"

"As often as I need to."

"Did you have a drink this morning?"

"No, but I wanted to."

"What stopped you?"

"I have some questions to ask you, and I need a clear head."

"Oh." He surprised her with his interest. "Well, go ahead and ask then. I'll do my best to answer."

He sat forward. "Besides the hacker who went rogue, have there been any other disgruntled patients of yours over the last few years?"

Audrey frowned and rubbed her temple. "Not that I recall."

"You have a headache?"

The pain in her head throbbed as if in answer. "I… Yes, a small one."

"Have you noticed any recent gaps in your memory? Fuzzy thoughts?"

She narrowed her gaze. "What are you suggesting?"

"Audrey, some of your memories have been wiped."

Her heartbeat sped up, and it felt like all the blood drained from her forehead at once. The room tilted in a crazy circle, and she saw white spots in front of her eyes. There was a rushing sound, and in an instant, all the colors in the room faded to black. She blinked and realized she was slumped in the recliner with Kevin leaning over her, shaking her shoulders, the earthy scent of him filling her nostrils.

"You okay?"

"Yes," she managed. Her skull felt like someone had stuffed it with cotton. "I…"

"You fainted. Take it easy." He crouched next to her, tucked a pillow behind her head, and helped her sit up. "I probably should have found a better way to tell you."

Ya think? What was even more shocking was him hovering over her like she was his patient. He needed to move far away so she didn't have to breathe in his rich, masculine smell. She had the insane desire to reach out and hug him so she'd feel safe.

Heat rushed to her cheeks, and her head cleared. "I'm…I'm all right now."

Kevin didn't budge, sending her blood pressure up a notch.

She brushed her hair behind her ears and tried to think. "You said my mind had been wiped. How can you know for certain?"

"I'm a former hacker, remember. I know the signs. What's more, your blocks have been removed."

"My blocks?" She sat forward, the hair on her arms rising with her. The blocks were for her safety—to protect her as she worked with hackers. "They're permanent. It's impossible to remove them…isn't it?"

He must have been reassured she had recovered from her faint because he stood and returned to the couch before answering, and she managed to get her breathing under control.

"Not quite. It's difficult for the vast majority of hackers, but not everyone."

"You mean you can do it," she said, hardly daring to breathe.

"Yes, and any other class tens who specialize in blocks. After all, we're the ones who put them in place. Audrey, I need you to think really hard about when you first started having headaches."

Audrey wrinkled her brow and considered. "Several years ago, maybe, but they seemed to get worse around the time Luke first arrived. That was about six months ago."

"Who's Luke?"

"The hacker who went rogue."

"Is Luke a class ten?"

"No, of course not. I don't work with class tens. You're the exception. Why are you glaring at me?"

Kevin had risen from the couch and was pacing. "If you don't normally work with class tens, don't you find it strange that you would be given an assignment to cure an incurable former hacker who *is* one?"

She sat forward. "Well, of course, I found it strange I was asked to work with you. I questioned it, but my boss didn't know the reason. He's new to the program and not well-versed in CMU policies. And for your information, I'm pretty good at what I do. I've had some success working with damaged hackers. Up until Luke, I had a fantastic reputation and was on my way to a promotion."

"Your reputation may be in shreds for a reason. Your memory loss isn't random. The person who removed your blocks knew what they were doing."

"Why would someone do this?"

"You must have witnessed something you shouldn't have. That would be the only reason to erase your memory. They could have removed your blocks to make you an easy target for hackers to invade your mind. If I had to hazard a guess, I'd say whoever's behind this caused Luke to go rogue so you'd be fired."

"But I was told I can come back if I'm able to cure you. Why would they give me the opportunity to return if they wanted me permanently gone?"

He clapped his hands together. "That's it! It's not counterintuitive because *you* can't cure me, and whoever this is knows it. They sent you here because they know you'll spend all your time trying. It's only an excuse to get you away from the situation. In the end you will fail, and you won't be able to return to the CMU. But in the meantime, you'll be out of the way."

She got up slowly. My God, it made a convoluted sense. A cold chill crawled down her spine, and she shivered. They had sent her here deliberately and didn't intend to give her job back. How would she ever earn the money she needed to meet her monthly expenses? Her mother would suffer because she couldn't get the care needed for severe stroke patients. Her sister would be a Harvard dropout.

She dropped her head in her hands. She didn't realize she was shaking until a pair of powerful arms encircled her, pulling her into a hard male chest.

Kevin's heartbeat settled in her ear—strong, steady, solid. Alarm bells rang in her head.

What are you doing, what are you doing, what are you doing?

It wasn't a major ethical violation to hug a patient, but something felt different about this hug, and she should probably push him away. But she couldn't seem to bring herself to do it. She curled her fingers into his shirt as if it were a familiar habit.

"Shh. It's okay. Lean on me. We'll figure this out together. You're not alone."

It took her a full minute to understand the words of comfort she heard were not spoken out loud but whispers in her mind. That fact, more than anything, had her loosening her grip and brushing him aside.

"You can talk to me in my head?"

He nodded and his cheeks reddened. "I apologize. It's second nature for me. I didn't even realize I was doing it. You have no blocks in place, and you're so emotional, it just happened." He held out his hands. "I promise, I was trying to help. I wasn't trying to invade your privacy."

She shook her head and swiped the tears rolling down her cheeks with the back of her hand. "I appreciated the hug…so thank you. It's been a good long while since I've had one." She tried to smile, but he saw too much. Knew too much. "It's not every day you discover your mind's been wiped, your blocks have been removed, and you're permanently unemployed."

She picked up her mug and strode into the kitchen more to get out from under the pity in his gaze than because she wanted a refill. She found the thermos and poured herself a cup of coffee, adding plenty of cream and sugar.

"You need money?"

"I…huh?" She had taken a sip of coffee and nearly spit it out. She found a paper towel and wiped her mouth. "Not for myself. But I do have some rather large expenses."

"Your mother and sister."

She moved toward him as if pulled by an invisible cord until she bumped into the couch where he lounged. "You've read that in my mind, I suppose?"

Why was that no longer shocking?

"Have a seat. I have something important to ask you."

She sat next to him, her nerves tingling.

"Audrey, I'd like to offer you a job."

Her heart thudded. "Why would you do that?"

Kevin's brow creased, and he looked genuinely puzzled. "You need money, and I need a therapist."

"But you told me you don't want a therapist…that you're incurable."

"That's true, but you told me you're really good at your job."

Insane laughter bubbled up and spilled out of her. She shook her head and stood. "I don't have to be a mind hacker to know when you're bullshitting. You don't want me as your therapist. You're offering me a job because you feel sorry for me."

She collected her purse and turned around, flinching when she found him standing behind her.

"You didn't strike me as a quitter, Doc." His voice was deep and low and sent shivers down her spine.

"I'm not a quitter." She pressed her lips together. "But I'm not stupid."

"I'll pay your wages, so it won't be a waste of your time. I know it doesn't look like I can afford to pay you, but I did well in my time with the CMU. You'll be well-compensated. You can continue taking care of your mom and sister."

"Why are you doing this? I know you don't really believe I can help you."

Silence stretched between them, and she didn't think he was going to answer until he did.

"Every hacker leaves a signature print in a target's mind when they wipe it. I believe I can find the hacker who did this to you if I can follow the trail. But I'm not well enough. Maybe you could teach me a few of those techniques you mentioned?"

CHAPTER SEVEN

Kevin watched Audrey drive off in the green Jeep, wondering if the lies he'd told would be enough to convince her to stick around. She had said she would think about it. In the meantime, it had been necessary to assess the damage in her mind and make sure she wasn't a government plant.

He turned and made his way into the dining room, his heart pounding as it had been doing since he'd made the discovery yesterday.

"What's wrong with you?" Hilda screeched.

"Not now, witch." He had far too much to think about. This afternoon, he'd confirmed what he'd only suspected yesterday: his own paranormal signature was all over the white patch in Audrey's mind. But he hadn't removed her mental blocks—that deed had been committed by another hacker.

Hilda was undeterred, thrusting her gnarled fingers at him. *"Do you have shit for brains?"*

Apparently, because he had no memory of wiping Audrey's mind—no memory of Audrey herself. How was it possible the accident had left him so damaged he couldn't remember anything about her or why he would have erased her memories?

He moved past Hilda and into the bedroom, where he sorted through his closet, looking for a decent pair of jeans. He'd obviously known her, but she had no memory of him—he'd checked.

He found a pair without rips or tears and pulled them off the hanger. Audrey had agreed to dinner at a pizza joint in town, where she promised to let him know if she'd accept his job offer.

"Think. Think. Think." The shadowy shapes seemed to be all around, whispering in his ears.

He changed his pants and ran his fingers through his hair, ignoring the fluttering in his stomach. If he had erased Audrey's memory, there must have been a good reason. Perhaps she'd been doing something illegal or stealing secrets for a foreign government? From the little he knew of her, she didn't strike him as a criminal or a spy.

"Don't you know anything? What's wrong with you?" Hilda wailed next to him. For a delusion, the hag could be pretty damn annoying.

He checked his phone—it was six p.m., and he wasn't meeting the doctor until seven, but he'd been trapped inside for too long and needed some air. He grabbed his wallet and keys, Hilda pursuing him out the door.

"You'll kill her."

"Shut up, Hilda." He got in the car and fastened his seatbelt, driving the short distance to downtown Marblehead. He didn't want to listen to the wicked witch of the west, but what if it were true? It was why he kept himself far away from everyone he knew and loved. He'd never understood what happened the day of the accident and how he'd managed to lose a portion of his memory. Had the voices buzzing in his ears caused him to snap? Would it happen again?

He parked in front of Lakehouse Pizza, turned off the engine, cracked the windows, and set the alarm for six forty-five. He'd wiped Audrey's mind, but there was no way he could have removed the blocks in her brain, since he'd been in Marblehead for the past few years. Someone else had accomplished that bit. Maybe the rogue hacker?

He shut his eyes and slowed his breathing, but he couldn't stop his thoughts or the headache that always followed the apparitions. It was like his brain was trying to make up for his missing memories.

After fifteen minutes of attempting to sleep, he quit trying and went into the restaurant.

***

Audrey walked toward the place Kevin told her made the best pizza in town, eyeing the many quaint storefronts lining each side of the street. Although it was only May and vacation season hadn't started, couples and families strolled up and down the sidewalk, chattering and walking their dogs. The sight was oddly reassuring.

She crossed the street and entered the crowded restaurant, searching for Kevin's larger-than-life presence. Her heart lurched when she spotted his familiar blond good looks at a table toward the back of the restaurant. Her knees grew weak, and her stomach twisted almost painfully.

She forced her legs forward. Her extreme reaction to the hacker's presence must be the reminder of her earlier shock, when he'd coolly told her someone had stolen her memories and that he could track the person.

Kevin hadn't looked up from the menu, which gave Audrey the chance to study him as she approached. He'd put on a bright blue shirt almost the exact shade of his eyes. He'd offered her a job as his therapist so he could go after the bad guy, but what if Kevin Jorgensen *was* the bad guy? Something about his request hadn't rung true. Yet, here she was, about to give her new patient the answer he was waiting to hear.

She swiped the hair from her eyes and took a breath. The man sitting in front of her so casually didn't look dangerous. But he could read her mind, erase her thoughts, and give her new ones if he chose. Had he implanted a thought this afternoon inducing her to accept his offer?

He glanced up as she neared the table and half-smiled. The adrenaline rush from seeing the look nearly stopped her heart. Why should a simple smile from a mentally ill recluse cause her heart to palpitate?

He stood up and pulled out her chair, and the gesture was so old-fashioned, she swallowed a lump in her throat. What was it about him that caused such a visceral reaction in her body?

"Are you hungry?"

"Yes."

"Good. I ordered for us. Pepperoni for me, and margherita for you."

No sooner had he spoken and the waitress arrived with two steaming pizzas. The tomatoey basil aroma caused her mouth to water—margherita was her favorite.

Wait a minute.

Their gazes locked across the table, and she sucked in air and blew it out. Without her mental blocks, slowing her breathing and heart rate was one of the best ways to keep the hacker out.

He flashed an apologetic smile and used the server to put two slices of margherita pizza on her plate. Knowing her favorite pizza was minor. What else had the hacker discovered about her? Was she the crazy one thinking she could work with a class ten talent without blocks in place?

He served himself three slices of pepperoni and wasted no time digging into them. Apparently, the man had an appetite.

"You've decided to accept my offer then?"

Breathe. One, two, three. Breathe.

She narrowed her gaze but kept her focus on her breathing and her mind blank, even though he'd clearly pulled her decision from her recent thoughts.

"Yes, but with a few stipulations."

"You expect me not to read your mind."

She met his knowing look with a hard one of her own. "Absolutely. I may be an open book to you right now, but as your therapist, I can't have you reading my every thought. I want a signed contract that states you will not read my mind unless I ask you to."

He nodded. "Agreed. And I'll go one further and restore the blocks that were removed."

"You…you will?"

"Yes." His mouthed creased into a thin, hard line, and she understood he was angry but not with her. "I can't risk restoring them in my current state. But I know someone who can."

"And you think I should trust this stranger who would do you a favor?"

"Yes, because if you've read my file, I'm sure you've seen his."

Ah. She stuck her straw in her soda and took a sip. "Your brother, Jordan."

"Yes. He's as honest as they come *and* a class ten."

Why would Kevin have his brother help her put her blocks back when it would be easier for him to read her without them?

Because he wants me to trust him.

He helped himself to another slice of pizza, which he polished off in three bites. "I can't have you walking around without blocks in place—it would be an invitation to every hacker out there. And whoever removed them obviously wants me to read your mind. I'd prefer not to cooperate."

His gaze caught hers, and she found she couldn't look away. "Despite what you think of me, I don't want to invade your privacy, which I will continually do *unintentionally.* Putting your blocks in place protects both of us."

Oh.

Something passed between them, some spark of recognition, and she understood him and his fear in a way she hadn't before.

It's not only about earning my trust.

She dropped her gaze to her plate, but she hardly noticed her food. Her new patient wasn't only trying to protect her from some unknown enemy in the CMU. That would be understandable, but that fact alone did not generate the worry in his gaze. No, he protected her from himself…feared he would harm her.

She lifted her chin and dug her nails into her palms. If she had any sense at all, she'd leave the restaurant, run like hell, and forget she'd ever met Kevin Jorgensen. But whatever good sense she possessed had fled along with her appetite. She needed to be outside in the open air.

He must have understood her intentions even as she thought them because he pulled three twenties from a leather wallet that looked like it had survived a war, laid them on the table, and stood.

"C'mon, I'll walk you home."

Kevin held the door open for Audrey and tried not to notice the way the yellow sundress accentuated her shape. Heat traveled up his spine and filled his lungs. Every time she was near him it was like basking in sunshine for the first time.

They stepped out on the sidewalk together and walked in the direction of the efficiency she'd rented. She didn't need to tell him where to go—he'd seen the memory of her apartment in her thoughts.

Audrey didn't look at him, but he could feel her focus and the fact she was trying to keep him out of her mind—a futile effort for someone with his talent. He needed to put her blocks in place and fast, because the more time he spent in her thoughts—accidental or otherwise—the more he craved a deeper connection.

"There's no need to walk me home. It's just a few blocks."

"I don't mind." And he didn't, which was strange when he thought about it. How could he feel so protective toward someone he'd deliberately harmed in the line of duty several years ago? Why did the thought of someone else hurting her anger him? Most disturbing of all, why did he look forward to her probing into his personal life as his therapist?

"I'll have the contract ready for you to sign tomorrow."

"Hmm, oh, right." *Ah, the contract.*

She might think it would protect her from his hacking into her mind, but no mere slip of paper would stop him. Without blocks in place, Kevin could be in and out of her brain so fast, Audrey would forget a contract even existed. That's why earlier today, he'd called Jordan, who he'd only seen once or twice since the accident. To his credit, his brother hadn't asked questions and agreed to help on the spot.

They had reached the place Audrey was renting and paused and turned toward each other as if in agreement.

"Come for breakfast tomorrow," he said. "I'll sign the contract."

"On one condition," she answered.

"What is it?"

She smiled—a genuine, breathtaking one. "I get to bring the coffee."

CHAPTER EIGHT

Audrey arrived at Kevin's house at eight o'clock the next morning, half expecting the hacker to be waiting at the door like last time. He was not. What's more, a strange car was parked in the drive.

She rang the bell and rang again. Had something happened to Kevin? Adrenaline coursed through her body. She had lifted her finger to lay on the bell once more when the door flung open and a stranger stared back at her. He had dark hair rather than blond, but other than that, he was a carbon copy of Kevin.

"You're Jordan, Kevin's brother."

"You're the doctor." Jordan didn't crack a smile, his eyes penetrating and distrustful. Hackers were notorious for being standoffish; she didn't take it personally.

"Yes, I'm your brother's new therapist, Audrey Gilbert."

"I see." He quirked a dark eyebrow, assessing. "A therapist who pays house calls?"

"My office is in Chicago, but I'm staying in Marblehead for the next few months."

He grunted, which Audrey took as a grudging acceptance. "What's in the thermos?"

Poison. "Coffee. Your brother's coffee-making skills are not the greatest, so I brought my own. You're welcome to try it."

He hesitated and stepped backward, allowing her to enter. "Here, let me."

Apparently, he'd had enough of his brother's coffee, too, because Jordan took the thermos from her and headed into the kitchen. Audrey followed, setting her stuff on the kitchen table and looking on as he poured them each a cup. He offered her one and picked up the other and took a tentative sip.

"It's good," he grunted. "Much better than the motor oil my brother calls coffee."

"Yes." She turned and found the cream and sugar and added generous amounts to her cup.

"I see you know your way around Kevin's kitchen."

She squinted at him. What was the hacker suggesting? "I know how to make myself a decent cup of coffee, if that's what you mean."

Jordan's expression smoothed, and his lips almost formed into a smile. "You've also made a positive impact on my brother."

She gave him her best you're-a-crazy-hacker look. "Where is Kevin?"

"In the shower."

Jordan turned, went into the dining room, and she followed.

"You know, I've rarely seen or spoken to Kevin since his accident five years ago," he said over his shoulder, "yet since you arrived, he's invited me here, there are no more beer cans strewn about, *and* he's taking a shower. Impressive."

"Thank you, but I can't take credit for any of these accomplishments, seeing as I've only been working with your brother for a few days."

"You're a miracle worker then." He turned and lifted his cup in the air. "To progress."

"To progress." She laughed and tilted her cup in his direction. She was beginning to understand Jordan's dry sense of humor and warm to him. "Are you here to restore my blocks? Your brother thought you could help."

Jordan nodded and made a disgusted face. "The sick bastard invited his only brother over for your sake and *not* because he missed me." He sat in the armchair, which left her the couch. "Why exactly are you missing your mental blocks?"

Audrey pressed her lips together. "I don't know. I didn't even know they were missing until yesterday when Kevin told me. Can you restore them?"

"Yes, it's now my specialty. It was Kevin's before the accident. He was something of a phenomenon in the field. I see you've read his file. You know he'd been working on a highly classified assignment when he was injured."

Audrey set her coffee cup on a small end table and sat a little straighter on the couch. She was getting used to these class tens reading her mind.

"What exactly happened to Kevin? You were there that day, weren't you?"

Jordan's expression grew grave. "You've read his file."

"I did. Please, it would really help me to understand a bit more about what your brother is going through emotionally. I can't get that from a file."

"Kevin doesn't like it when I talk about his accident."

"Kevin's not here at the moment, though, is he?"

"True." Jordan scratched his chin, his green eyes taking on an assessing look. "We were in the mind of the wife of a Chinese diplomat, Li Sue Yeh. It was supposed to be a simple job—search her mind for evidence and retreat. Unfortunately, a rogue hacker had already wiped Li Sue Yeh's mind and set a trap so she would awaken while we were inside. The lead hacker had to eject the entire team from her mind unexpectedly."

"Kevin got caught in the cross waves?"

"Yes. He was the last out, and he lost a piece of himself in Li Sue Yeh's mind that day. At first, we thought he was fine. He suffered only a slight memory loss but seemed to recover and was back on the job within a month. He began working on another assignment—one he wouldn't tell me about."

"And then…?" she prompted when the silence stretched between them.

Jordan let out a gusty sigh. "And then Kevin's memory loss worsened. He missed whole segments of time. He grew elusive and bitter and wouldn't talk to anyone, not even me. He started seeing therapists, one after another. None of them seemed to be able to get to the root of the problem. Eventually, Kevin quit the CMU and moved to Marblehead."

"He gave up."

"Yes, and there's not a day goes by I don't worry about him. Do you think you can help my brother?"

Audrey met Jordan's gaze directly. "I'm not sure. He has to want to be helped first."

Jordan raised his eyebrows. "He hasn't talked to any other therapist in years. That fact alone tells me he sees you differently than the others. You might be able to reach him."

"According to the file, your brother suffers 'psychotic episodes'. Have you been with him when he's had one?"

Jordan pursed his lips like he tasted something rotten, but Audrey didn't think it was the coffee. "Yes."

"Tell me about it."

"It was after he had recovered from the accident. I went to visit him in his apartment in Cleveland. When I got there, he was acting strangely, looking over his shoulder, jumping at every sound. He looked like he hadn't slept in weeks."

"Maybe he was over tired? None of those symptoms mean he's psychotic."

"I thought that, too, since he'd been involved in this big secret project for the CMU. But he plucked a knife from a kitchen drawer and waved it in the air like it was a light saber. He yelled like he was fighting for his life. It was everything I could do to get him to calm down and get the knife away from him."

"Do you remember what he was saying?"

"I'll never forget it. He screamed, 'Back off, bitch', like someone was attacking him."

"Why wasn't this incident noted in the official file?"

"I didn't report it, that's why. I didn't want my brother locked away. The CMU has ways of dealing with hackers who lose their shit on the job, and they're not pretty."

"I see."

"What do you see?" Kevin Jorgensen stood shirtless in the dining room entrance, rubbing his hair with a towel. From the steam in his voice, he was about ready to blow his stack.

"Take it easy, bro. Your therapist was just asking for my opinions on your condition."

Kevin shrugged into his shirt, and despite the frost in the gaze he shot her way, Audrey managed to swallow.

"Doesn't the patient have to be present during therapy sessions, Doc? Or is this some sort of unorthodox method you employ to get yours to confide in you?"

"Of course, it's not. I merely…"

"Let me be clear, I don't want my family drawn into this mess."

If he would take a dislike to you, he could do some serious damage…maybe take your life.

Audrey shivered at the fierceness in Kevin's tone.

"Kevin…" Jordan stepped in front of Audrey.

Years of working with distressed hackers came to her rescue, and Audrey straightened her shoulders and moved around Jordan, adopting her most professional tone.

"As your therapist, it's important I understand the full extent of your injuries."

Kevin's eyes flared, his gaze locked with hers, and a tingle moved down her spine.

Jorgensen is a recluse and unstable.

Her boss's warning echoed in Audrey's mind.

"Might I remind you as your soon-to-be new employer that we need to focus on restoring your blocks, Doc? Which is why I invited Jordan to join us. You'll have plenty of time to psychoanalyze me later."

He'll resent your intrusion on his solitude.

Her boss was right. Her new patient didn't want therapy—he was only interested in restoring her mental blocks and finding the hacker who had erased her memory.

Bingo.

Audrey heard the word clearly in her head and gasped. If Kevin wanted to illustrate why she needed mental blocks, the single word did the trick.

He smiled coolly and gestured toward the manila folder on the kitchen table. "Isn't that my contract? Why don't I look it over so we can get down to work?"

CHAPTER NINE

Kevin read the single-page agreement and tried not to hear the thoughts of the woman across from him.

Superiority complex…reclusive asshole…mistake.

That about summed up their relationship. Everything she thought about him was true. So why did he let it bother him?

He focused on the language in the document. It seemed pretty standard. He must restore her mental blocks and avoid entering her mind uninvited. She agreed to act as his therapist in exchange for a reasonable hourly rate. If either of them failed to meet the terms of the agreement, the document was null and void.

He signed the contract without hurrying and set down his pen. Despite what Audrey thought of him, he didn't want to hurt her.

He glanced up to meet her gaze. He could drown in those soft gray eyes—they seemed to penetrate his own.

"She's lovely, but you can't have her," Hilda cackled in his ear. *"You can never have her."*

"Kevin, what is it?"

He shook his head. If he told Audrey about Hilda, it would only make her more determined to help him. And no one could stop the hallucinations.

"It's time to reinstall your blocks." He turned to Jordan, who was stretched out on the couch. "Are you ready?"

Jordan yawned and stood. "Sure, but the bigger question is Kevin…are you?"

"What do you mean?" Audrey asked. "Is it dangerous?"

"Not for you," Jordan said, coming into the kitchen and putting his coffee cup in the sink. "But there's always a danger for hackers."

"Will it hurt?"

"It might make the headaches worse for a time," Kevin said.

"Wait a minute…what did Jordan mean by hackers? You're not both…"

"Take it easy. He meant hackers in general. I'm not planning to install your blocks—that's why Jordan's here. Once the blocks are in place, you and I will get down to work."

"Kevin, I know you don't believe I can help you, but once my blocks are in place, you will let me try, won't you?"

"You think she can help you?" Hilda screamed in his ear. *"No one can help you. You're damaged beyond repair. Damaged goods. Damaged goods. Damaged goods."*

"She's lovely, lovely, lovely," the shadows whispered, their voices hanging in the air.

"She's in danger." Abe groaned. *"Keep her with you."*

"Kevin? Did you hear what I said? I want to have a therapy session with you as soon as my blocks are in place." Audrey was giving him that something's-wrong-but-I'm-not-sure-what look again.

He shrugged and clenched his fists. "We'll see."

"Are you ready to get started?" Jordan asked Audrey.

"What do I need to do?"

"Lay down on the couch. You're gonna want to sleep afterwards."

She did as Jordan asked, and Kevin found himself caring for her like she was a child—tucking a pillow under her head and laying a blanket over her prone form. "You ready?"

"Is all this really necessary?"

He tried for a reassuring smile. "Yes." He lodged a command in her brain with a single thrust. "Sleep now."

Audrey slept.

"What is it?"

A conversation was going on in the next room, but Audrey couldn't figure out who was speaking. Her head was being squeezed in a vise, and her throat was parched. She tried to roll over but got tangled in the blanket.

Where am I?

The voices continued.

"Some kind of special portal, I think."

"Our doctor must be valuable for the CMU to install a portal in her mind. Why do you think they did it?"

"They're using her to get to me. Every single one of her blocks had been removed. They knew I'd read her mind and keep her around."

The voices were clearer now, and the fog in Audrey's head lifted. She was lying on a couch in Kevin's house, which meant the voices belonged to Kevin and Jordan.

She tried to sit up, moaning at the stabbing sensation in her skull. What had they done to her?

"Shhh, take it easy, Audrey." Kevin came over from the kitchen and knelt beside her, placing a cool hand on her forehead. "She's not running a fever. Here, drink this."

He held a cold glass of water against her lips, and she managed to take a sip. The scent of his earthy cologne floated up to her, and she moaned again, leaning into his chest before she knew what she was doing.

He wrapped his arms around her. "It will get better, I promise. Your mind has to get used to the blocks again."

"I don't remember it hurting this bad the first time around."

"That's because there weren't blank spots the first time," Jordan said. "You're missing a quite a few memories. I had to work around that."

Kevin grunted and moved away, the softness he had shown her vanishing, replaced by suspicion. "You also have something implanted in your mind."

She licked dry lips and tried to make sense of what he was saying. "The portal?"

The brothers glanced at each other.

"You heard us talking," Kevin said. "Did you know about this?"

"No, I swear. Did you remove it?" She pressed her fingers against the ache in her temples.

Kevin shook his head, his expression grim. "No, Jordan tried."

She caught another quickly exchanged look between the brothers. "Why is it there?"

Kevin didn't answer but stood and walked into the bathroom, leaving Jordan to explain. "It's a plant," Jordan said.

"A what? You mean like a bug?"

"Sort of. More like a way for another hacker to get into your head."

"My God." A cold trickle of fear moved down her spine. "You mean whoever installed this can enter my mind at will? Why would that be necessary?"

Kevin returned with two pills and handed them to her. "You'll thank me later."

"What are these?"

"Aspirin for the headache. Take two and call me in the morning, Doc."

If he was trying to make her smile, it worked. She downed the pills and drank more water.

"Jordan, why would a hacker want to spy on me?"

Jordan grimaced. "The government sent you to work with Kevin, a high-profile hacker. No offense, but I don't think the government is interested in your day-to-day doings."

"You're saying they're trying to get to Kevin through me?"

"Yeah, that's it," Jordan said. "He's a class ten talent, and he'd been working on something so secret before the accident, even he doesn't fully remember it. He might have discovered something, which they may be hoping he reveals to you."

"Well then, you gotta find a way to take it out."

"That's just it. I can't remove it. It appears to be tuned to the paranormal signature of another hacker."

CHAPTER TEN

"*Why are you lazing in bed, you no good scum?*" Hilda woke him up the next morning by screaming in his ear.

He moaned and rolled over, but the hag was relentless.

"*Get up, get up, get up. You know what you need to do.*"

Yes, he knew, but that didn't mean he wanted to think about it. He hadn't tried to emulate another hacker's paranormal signature for years. It required extreme control. What if he hurt Audrey?

He rubbed his eyelids and checked the time on his watch—six a.m. He hadn't had his usual dose of beer the past few nights, which could explain his racing pulse and intense anxiety. If only he could be certain he would remain steady when he was inside Audrey's mind. If only he knew there would be no hallucinations.

He rolled out of bed, slipped on the pair of jeans he'd worn yesterday, and selected a fresh shirt from his closet. Would she bring her own coffee this morning?

He headed to the bathroom for deodorant and cologne. He didn't stop to analyze why it was so important he look and smell clean, but he told himself it wasn't motivated by his pretty therapist.

He studied the new growth of whiskers on his face in the mirror and picked up the razor. He needed a haircut. Would she still find him as attractive as she had yesterday? He frowned at his reflection. Why was it all thoughts returned to her?

After he shaved, he made his way into the kitchen and studied the coffee pot. He bet she'd taste as good as her coffee. Would he get another chance to hold her? A jolt of excitement moved through his body, and he had to take a moment to slow his breathing to avoid projecting his thoughts to his brother, who was asleep on the sofa.

"Why bother?" Jordan yawned and stretched. "I've already heard dozens of your projections. You've got it bad, bro."

Kevin stilled. "What the hell are you talking about?"

Jordan popped his head up from the couch and grinned. "You've got the hots for your sexy little therapist. Don't bother trying to deny it. I saw the way you two looked at each other yesterday, and you weren't the only one to hear her thoughts."

Jordan raised his voice an octave. "'His eyes are so blue. He smells amazing. I want to crawl inside his shirt.' Blaah. No wonder you're showering and shaving and calling your only brother for help when you haven't for the past five years."

Kevin rolled his eyes. "Yeah, about that. I have my reasons."

Jordan ambled into the kitchen, rubbing a hand through his bedhead. He stopped to stare at the coffee pot with Kevin. "I know your reasons, and I've respected them. But I think they no longer matter."

Kevin frowned. "What do you mean?"

Jordan sighed. "If you're contemplating entering her mind to remove the portal, Kev, you've got yourself under control. You would never do it otherwise. Do you think she'll bring more coffee?"

Kevin's heart rate accelerated, and no amount of deep breathing exercises could calm it. "I'm counting on it."

<hr>

Audrey arrived at Kevin's door a few hours later with a box of donuts and a thermos of coffee.

"Donuts?" Kevin asked when he answered the door and spotted the white carton. His eyes looked bluer than normal, if that were possible. A robin's-egg blue—like the sky in springtime.

She nodded and managed a smile.

"Allow me."

Audrey's hand shook a little when she handed him the items and their fingers brushed. There had to be a rule somewhere about being attracted to your patient, but she'd never had it happen before, so she wasn't sure.

"What's all this?" She frowned and pointed at the drawn curtains and the pills and glass of water on a table next to the couch.

Kevin didn't answer. He and Jordan were already on their way into the kitchen to pour themselves a cup of the hot brew.

She raised her voice. "Hey, what's with the aspirin?"

"They're for you," Kevin said, returning to the dining room with a chocolate donut in one hand and a cup of coffee in the other, which he set on the table in front of her. "Have a seat. Want a donut?"

"Oh, no." She smiled. "Thanks for the coffee. I had a donut earlier. My headache's much better."

"You're going to need all the ammunition you can get for today's exercise," Jordan said, coming into the room and clutching his own donut and cup of coffee.

"Today's exercise?" She turned to Kevin, who handed her the glass of water. "Why do I suddenly feel like I'm the patient and you guys are the therapists?"

Jordan looked at Kevin. "Do you want to tell her or shall I?"

Adrenaline coursed through her system, and her stomach sank. "I knew you two were keeping secrets yesterday with all your covert glances at one another. Spill."

Kevin sat next to her, sending her heart rate into overdrive. "Audrey, I'm going to need to break the terms of our contract."

Audrey moved to the edge of the couch and gripped the seat cushion. "Already? You only signed it yesterday."

"Yeah, but that was before we told you there was a portal placed in your mind by another hacker."

"You claimed only the hacker who put the device in place could remove it."

"That is true with one exception."

She narrowed her gaze. "You?"

He nodded and looked straight ahead, as if he were afraid to see her reaction. "Before I left the CMU, I had been working on a process to identify the paranormal signatures of hackers. Originally, the plan was to capture the signatures so that they could be catalogued. But I discovered, quite by accident, I could often replicate them."

"Wait a minute. Are you saying you could replicate the signature of the unknown hacker who planted the portal in my brain?"

"I'm saying I *may* be able to—and the procedure is not without risk."

"He's being modest," Jordan said. "He's not worried about replicating the hacker's signature. Kevin is an expert in the field."

Her gaze locked with Kevin's. "What *are* you worried about, then?"

Kevin didn't answer and the silence between them was heavy with secrets.

It was Jordan who finally grew impatient with his brother and provided an explanation. "He's worried he's going to lose his shit while he's in your mind."

Kevin rolled his eyes. "You have such a wonderful bedside manner, Jordan."

"Why don't you tell me a little about what you experience when you lose it?" Audrey asked him, in full therapist mode.

Kevin clasped his hands together and growled his frustration. "Now's not the time to psychoanalyze me, Doc. Save that for your next victim."

"We already know my blocks were removed, part of my memory was erased, and now there is a portal. If you expect me to let you agree to waltz into my mind, poke around, and potentially jeopardize my mental health, forget it. Why should I take the risk if I can't reassure myself you're healthy enough to do the deed?"

Kevin dragged a hand through his hair. "Because someone can use the portal implanted in your mind to spy on you, and I'm the only one who can possibly remove it, that's why."

"Don't screw this up," Hilda hissed into his ear. *"You'll destroy her."*

He clenched his jaw. What if he damaged Audrey beyond repair? But if he left the portal in her mind, her privacy was at risk. Whoever installed it could enter and leave her mind at will. The government could be spying on them now.

"She's got a valid point, Kev."

"Fine. But I don't need an audience." He glared at Jordan, who didn't seem to take offense.

"Sure, bro. Call me when you've made progress." He waved a hand in the air and headed out the front door. "Bye, Audrey."

After Jordan left, Audrey found her notebook and pen and began to scribble.

Why did shrinks always write everything down? Kevin hadn't even said anything important. "What are you doing?"

"Hmm?"

He rolled his eyes. "What are you writing in your notebook about me?"

"I'm capturing a few observations."

He made an exasperated sound, and she lifted her stormy gaze to meet his. How was it every time he looked at her, he wanted to pull her into his arms and never let her go? With her blocks in place, he could no longer hear her thoughts, which should be a relief but wasn't. He wanted to know what she was thinking.

"How about you put the notebook aside and ask me your questions instead."

She hesitated. "A psychiatrist's job is to observe and record what they see and hear. It helps us structure a treatment plan."

"No, it makes the person feel ill at ease and like any other patient."

Their gazes locked, and the energy in the air increased to a record level. What would she do if he pulled her to him and kissed her smooth cheeks and her mouth and explored her neck and every bit of skin he could reach?

"Take it slow. It's been a while." Jesus. Abe loomed over her, nodding and bringing Kevin back to reality faster than a cold shower.

Audrey's gaze narrowed, and she put the notebook aside and clasped her fingers together in her lap. "All righty then. Why don't you tell me about the episodes you've been experiencing?

He dug his fingers into his palms. What would she think of him after he told her the truth? Would she consider him damaged goods, unfit for a relationship? He wasn't good enough for her in his current state. He knew that. But what if it were possible to put an end to the annoying hallucinations? For the first time in a long time, he wanted to try.

He rested his head against the couch cushions and shut his eyes. "I'm visited often by people who aren't really there. I hear whispers in my head. I don't know what else you want to hear."

"What do your visitors say?"

"Mostly they scold me, remind me of things I'd rather forget."

"Like what?"

"Like…" He thought back to Hilda's rant this morning. "I'm forgetful, I'm stupid, I don't deserve to live."

"Do you believe what they tell you?"

"Sometimes, yes. I messed up." He still hadn't opened his eyes. It was easier that way.

"You didn't mess up, Kevin. You have a dangerous job, and as a class ten talent, I'm sure you were given the toughest assignments. You couldn't be expected to be perfect every time."

She leaned toward him, and he felt it in his soul.

"She's lovely, she's lovely, she's lovely." The shadows were all around, whispering.

"Listen, I'd like to try something with you. It's a mild regression technique I've used successfully with patients who have experienced similar hallucinations. It will require a light stage of hypnosis. Would you be willing?"

He opened his eyes. She was so damn beautiful it hurt. He could only place a hand over his heart and move his head up and down dumbly.

"Great." She smiled and touched his arm.

It was only the barest touch, but it left heat in its wake. *Her* heat.

"Now, here's what I need you to do. Close your eyes, and I'll walk you through a guided meditation. The goal is to get to know your visitors, find out what drives them."

"What drives them is to drive me batty," he grumbled, but there wasn't any anger. He'd do any guided meditation she wanted to offer so long as he could hear her melodic voice and have her sitting next to him.

"Okay then. I want you to imagine you are in a sunny place—somewhere you feel warm and safe."

He imagined they were sitting on a beach together. She had on a straw hat and sunglasses and the sexiest black bikini he'd seen in some time. They were together—a couple—holding hands as the heat from the sun and the cool breeze kissed their skin.

"You're content and sleepy. Your mind is drifting. You see one of your visitors. Who is it?"

"Abe." Abe was hovering over him, glowering, a warning look in his eyes.

"What does Abe want to tell you?"

"Be careful. You'll lose her."

"Lose who?"

"The woman you love most in the world."

CHAPTER ELEVEN

"You understand now? Abe and Hilda and all the other hallucinations you see are a part of you."

Audrey cleared her throat, which had grown tight, and stared at the notebook in her lap. Kevin had awakened from hypnosis but still sat next to her on the couch, and she hadn't fully recovered from the shock of his announcement.

The woman you love most in the world.

How could she have such intense feelings for someone who loved another?

"What are you thinking?"

Her cheeks grew hot. Had she projected her thoughts?

Strong fingers grasped her chin and raised it until she met his gaze. She blinked and hoped her blocks held.

"Thank you," he said, and her heart trembled. "I hadn't realized until now that the hallucinations are trying to get me to remember."

"Yes, and the trauma you experienced is because you lost someone important to you…someone you lov…loved." She stumbled over the words and blinked, so he wouldn't see the sudden tears, which rushed to her burning eyes.

My God, I'm falling for him.

The sick feeling in the pit of her stomach wasn't caused by the donut she'd devoured this morning.

He smiled and brushed a tear from the corner of one eye. "Whoever the mysterious woman I love is, she can't hold a candle to you, Doc."

He leaned forward and brushed his lips across hers, and she suspected she was breaking every law in the books when she kissed him back.

And what a kiss it was…unlike anything she'd ever experienced. His kiss was soft and rugged and all-consuming, and the taste of him was more addicting than the vanilla creamer she put in her coffee every morning.

She moaned as his lips brushed her earlobes, the column of her throat, and her chest. He pressed her against him so tightly she could smell his sweat and the sandalwood in his cologne. She felt the beating of his heart, which seemed to beat in time with hers.

When was the last time she'd been held like this? She'd been so focused on her career, she hadn't dated anyone, and she'd never kissed a patient this way before.

A patient…he's a patient.

The words rang in her head, cutting through the dense fog in her brain.

"Don't think," Kevin muttered, his hands tangling in her hair.

But it was too late. She had thought, and she had just enough sense to push him away. "I'm sorry, Kevin, but this is wrong."

And it was wrong on so many levels. First, it was a severe breach of medical ethics. If it became known she'd kissed her patient, and in his home to boot, she'd lose her license. Second, he was in love with another woman.

"Audrey." Her name sounded like a prayer, and he caressed her cheek with the back of his hand until she trembled. "This *is* right…the most right I've felt in ages. Forget about the unknown woman. It's you I want."

"No, Kevin. It's *not* me you want, it's *her*. I've seen this before in my practice. Hackers who are so relieved I've helped them deal with their trauma that they fixate on me. You don't really want *me*—you're grateful, is all."

"Audrey…"

She brushed his hand away and stood. "Now that you've associated the 'hallucinations' you've been experiencing with your missing memories, you'll remember more. Eventually, you'll remember everything—you'll remember what happened the day of the accident. You'll remember who she is and why you fell in love with her."

And once he remembered, he would want to forget he'd ever kissed Audrey.

I'm his doctor, nothing more.

He stood, towering over her, close enough she could feel the rhythm of his breathing. "I can't remember something that isn't there. My memories were wiped, not buried. What can I do to make you believe I want you for yourself and not because of some silly hypnotic technique?"

She stood as straight as she could, but she still had to look up to see his face. "It's not silly. You do have memories buried in your mind. I know that now. Work with me to restore them. If you still want me afterwards, then I'll believe you."

"Deal." He held out his hand and waited for her to shake it. When she did, he threaded his fingers between hers and pulled her closer, until she could feel his body heat.

"I will still want you, Audrey. No matter what happens, no matter who I remember. I swear it."

Kevin pressed his pillow around his ears and did his best to shut out the voices.

"You let her go. Why'd you let her go?" Abe moaned.

Ever since Abe's earlier revelation under hypnosis, he'd become the dominant hallucination in Kevin's head. Hilda had grown strangely quiet—he couldn't say he missed her.

"You act like I had a choice. I didn't want to let her go." Did it mean he'd lost it if he was talking back to the hallucination?

He turned over and buried his face in the pillow. After Audrey issued her challenge, she'd agreed to have him try to remove the portal in her brain. The procedure would take under an hour.

"You can't make a mistake. You'll lose her." The whispers were driving him insane. Or perhaps they'd already made him insane.

He squeezed his eyes shut and went over the task again. Jordan would shut down Audrey's blocks, Kevin would enter her mind, duplicate the paranormal signature of the hacker who installed the portal, and remove it. If all went well, he would exit Audrey's mind, and Jordan would reinstall her blocks.

"I have a bad feeling about this," Abe groaned.

"Yeah, buddy, I do, too. You and the others need to keep it down for that one hour. Please."

"Be careful. Be careful. Be careful."

Kevin turned on the radio to drown out the voices and fell asleep to the sound of sweet jazz music and thoughts of his therapist.

***

"Are you ready? You'll sleep like last time."

Audrey rested her head on the couch cushion and nodded, wondering if she would suffer the headaches afterward. Was she the crazy one to put herself under the care of her patient? But she didn't want the government spying on her, and she trusted Kevin not to harm her. Besides, Jordan was there to keep an eye on things.

"Sleep then," Kevin said.

Audrey slept and dreamt.

The blinds in her office at the Corvey Institute were drawn low, and a patient lay in the recliner across from her, eyes closed. "How are you feeling today, Luke?"

She had placed him in a light stage of hypnosis. They were close to unlocking the secrets in his mind.

"Great, Doctor. You were right when you said the flashbacks I've been having are pieces of my own memories."

She smiled, knowing Luke had discovered what she'd understood from the start. He'd built a virtual safe in his mind that only he could open…if he could find the key. That was her role as his therapist in the experiment.

"Why do you believe this, Luke?" If she could help him open the box at will, the Ignotus project would have done what no outfit had done before: They would have created a lock and key to a virtual safety deposit box in the human mind. Hackers would no longer need to guard the minds of the country's brightest scientists, inventors, and government officials. They would simply install the box to safeguard their secrets and access it when needed.

"Because the flashbacks are trying to get my attention. My subconscious mind is working to help me recall what's missing," Luke said.

"Very good. Now, I want you to imagine you are walking down a hallway, and there are doors in your mind. Each door leads to a different memory. Can you see the doors?"

"Yes," Luke intoned.

"Are they locked?"

"No, they're open…except for one."

"What does it look like?"

"It's at the end of the hallway, and it's larger than the rest. The handle won't budge."

"Can you see the lock?"

"Yes."

"Describe it to me."

"It's a dial that needs a combination. I can't open it."

"Yes, you can, Luke. You've written the combination down and stored it somewhere. You just have to remember where you stored it."

"Yes."

"Can you remember?"

"Yes, it's under the mat."

Excitement drove a scorching path through her veins. They were so close now. She could taste victory. "Find the combination, Luke. Use it to unlock the door."

"I found it."

"Enter the combination. Have you done that?"

"Yes."

"Turn the handle and tell me what's inside."

"Holy crap." Luke gasped and sat up, breathing hard.

A buzzing sounded in her left ear, growing louder and louder until it was almost painful. Audrey cracked her eyes open to see two concerned faces leaning over her. She flung up a hand in reaction.

"What's wrong? You have a headache?" Kevin asked, gripping her flailing hand in his warm ones, his touch gentle but his voice tenser than she'd ever heard it. He smoothed a piece of hair that had fallen into her eyes and tucked it behind her ear.

She wrinkled her nose. The pain she had become so used to feeling at her temples was noticeably absent. "No, but I remembered something…something I can't believe I'd forgotten."

"I know."

"How?" Audrey tried to sit.

"Don't move," Kevin said, gripping her hands to hold her in place like she was fragile, his intense blue eyes blazing into hers.

"Why are you freaking out? I feel fine."

"He's freaking out because he just accomplished something rare in the hacking world. Not only did he remove the portal, but he restored a piece of memory hidden behind it. The next half hour is critical to make sure there's no damage. So lie still, unless you want to give my brother a heart attack."

Her stomach cramped. "That's why I remembered." What else was missing from her mind?

"Yeah," Kevin muttered. "Hell, don't cry." He huffed out a breath. "If I knew it would hurt you, I wouldn't have done it."

"No, I'm…I'm just…" She sighed, her breathing ragged. "It's overwhelming knowing that someone implanted that portal thing in my mind and stole my memories. What other memories am I missing? This is awful."

He brushed her cheek. "I know, sweetheart. I wish I could give them all back to you."

"I'm off to take care of the business we talked about," Jordan said. He smiled at Audrey. "You're in good hands with my brother."

Kevin nodded, but he didn't lift his gaze from Audrey, and she hardly knew what was happening between them. "What was it you remembered?"

She suspected he asked the question only to distract her from crying, but she told him about Luke anyway. "I remembered the patient, Luke, who I thought *wasn't* a class ten, *was* one. He didn't have a mental health issue at all. He and I had been working on a special project for a government outfit called Ignotus. We were attempting to install a virtual safe in his mind and open it later." She narrowed her gaze. "Why don't you look shocked by any of this?"

He gave her a crooked smile. "I was in your mind, remember? I remembered it with you. I wasn't trying to pry. I needed to make certain there were no hidden surprises buried in the memory."

"But don't you see what this means? Luke wouldn't have gone rogue because of something I did.

He didn't *have* any mental health issues. Someone else must have caused him to lose it."

"I know. Jordan's on his on his way to Chicago now. We'll get to the bottom of this, I promise."

"There's something else I still don't understand, though. Why would the government send me to you, knowing you could duplicate the paranormal signature of the hacker who installed the portal and remove it?"

Kevin's blue eyes glittered. "They didn't know I could duplicate signatures. I never told anyone. And after my accident there were gaps in my memory and I was hallucinating. If they knew what I was capable of, they wouldn't have asked questions. They would have locked me up. The only person I ever told was Jordan, and he swore to keep it a secret."

She rested her fingers over his heart. "I will keep your secret, too."

He brought her fingers to his lips. "I know."

CHAPTER TWELVE

Audrey helped herself to a glass of water in Kevin's kitchen and tried to keep her hand from shaking. "What is it?" She might not be a mind hacker, but she'd felt his presence behind her on a cellular level. And she understood something he resisted and didn't fully comprehend yet. She turned and plastered on the most natural smile she could muster. "Nothing. Are you hungry?"

He took the glass from her trembling fingers and set it on the counter. Then he pulled her into his arms and held her.

"What is it?" He whispered the words in her ear and kissed the top of her head. "Are you thinking about her again? The woman I supposedly love? You're all I want."

She couldn't contain the shiver that racked her body.

He lifted his head enough to see her face. "Audrey, sweetheart, are you really going to let a phantom woman stand between us?"

She took a breath. "You are like Luke."

He glowered at her, his body stiffening.

Her pulse raced and she pulled away. "Kevin, Luke's a victim the same as me."

He let out a gusty sigh. "I didn't want to have to tell you this."

"Tell me what?"

"Jordan texted a half hour ago. He got word Luke is dead—apparent suicide. We believe your good friends at Ignotus killed Luke, which they would have only done because he could rat them out. Now that the portal is removed, they don't have a way to use your mind to get to mine. Luke was no longer useful to them."

She creased her brow. "They killed Luke because he's the one who installed the portal in my mind? Is he also responsible for my missing memories?"

Kevin's expression didn't change but something in his eyes shifted, raising the hair on her arms. He shook his head. "Luke installed the portal and hid your memory of him, but he didn't erase your other memories. I did."

Her heart skipped a beat, and she couldn't take in enough oxygen. "Why would you do that?"

"I don't know. And believe me, it's killing me. I may never know why. It's part of my missing memories. But you must have seen something you shouldn't have. That would be the only thing I can think of."

And suddenly she knew the truth.

The room swayed. She lost her balance and would have fallen if he wasn't holding her up. The answer was in the details, and the details were trapped within his mind.

She pulled in air and straightened her spine. She had feelings for him. And because she cared for him she could do this, even though she would lose him when he learned the truth. The thought of what would be lost before it had a chance to take root and grow hurt to contemplate.

"Your memories aren't missing, Kevin. You have a virtual safe like Luke's buried in your mind. And I can help you open it."

Kevin could see the hurt in her eyes and read the truth in her mind, even with the blocks in place. She thought he loved a phantom. That she would open the safe in his mind, and he would leave her.

He pulled her closer. He didn't care what memories the safe held, he'd never let her go.

She snuggled next to his heart, where she belonged.

For the first time in his life, Kevin wished someone else could read his mind and know what he felt. He'd never been much good at expressing his deeper feelings, and the accident had destroyed something in his make-up. But there was another way to let her know what she'd come to mean to him in a short time.

He pulled her into his arms and kissed her, and she sighed and melted into him. *Mission accomplished.*

Kissing Audrey was like circling the sun and moon and stars all at once. She blasted him out of orbit.

He licked the saltiness of her tears and did what he could to distract her from her lonely thoughts. And she let him for a time. But eventually, as he'd known she would, she pushed him away. Because his phantom lover stood between them.

"We need to open the safe, Kevin."

He sighed and rested his forehead against hers. "Now?"

"Ye…yes." Her voice wobbled.

He sighed again. How he hated that she hurt. It was like hurting a piece of himself. "Okay, then. What do you need me to do?"

They returned to the couch, which had gotten a steady workout over the past week. She had him close his eyes, as she'd had Luke do in her memory.

"You don't want to lose her." Was it his imagination, or was Hilda's voice less strident than normal?

"Picture a set of stairs," Audrey said. "With each step, you will go deeper and deeper into sleep. You will feel your body grow heavier and heavier. One. When you reach the bottom of the stairs, you will be in a deep, deep sleep. Two. You will not wake up until I say, 'wake.' Three. You will be so tired, so heavy. Four. You see the bottom of the stairs. Your limbs are heavy, you can't move them. Your body is so sleepy. Five. You're asleep now."

"This way." Abe pointed down a long hallway.

There were the doors as Kevin had seen in her memory with Luke. The large yellow door at the end of the hallway glistened and beckoned. He studied the giant padlock. It needed a skeleton key to unlock, and he remembered where he'd left it.

He reached above the giant door and found the key. He studied the gold surface and the many crevices, fit the key into the lock, twisted. The door slid smoothly on its hinges and opened.

Audrey knew the moment he remembered. It was exactly like the last time with Luke. Except she hadn't experienced these intense feelings for Luke. She hadn't hurt inside watching him remember.

Kevin sat up and opened his eyes like he'd seen a ghost. But he didn't see her. He was still in a trance, reacquainting himself with the memories he'd lost several years ago.

He smiled, and the sight caused Audrey's heart to stutter and quake until she had to look away. He was remembering her—whoever *she* was—her competition for his heart.

And he must have seen all the memories there were to see because he lay back down, and Audrey brought him to a waking state.

She found her notebook and documented the details, trying not to fall apart.

Kevin opened his eyes and looked for Audrey. She sat in the armchair across from him writing in her notebook—notes about him.

He cleared his throat. "Audrey, I remember everything."

She didn't glance his way, her pen scratching the page.

The voices were blessedly silent for once.

He sat up. "Audrey, look at me, please."

Now she did look at him, but her gaze was distant. The woman he had thoroughly kissed an hour or two ago had vanished and in her place was a professional therapist.

"Since you've recovered your memories, you'll probably notice the hallucinations you had been experiencing have disappeared. I'm glad for you, of course."

She got up and moved toward the door. "I've completed my notes, and I'll write you a clean bill of health. You'll be able to return to your former life, resume your previous job, relationships."

He stood and moved toward her. "Aren't you going to ask me *what* I had forgotten?"

She shook her head, not looking at him, her hair partially hiding the tears glistening on her cheeks. "There is no reason for me to kn…know."

He plucked the notebook from her grasp, tossed it aside, and pulled her into his arms. At first, she resisted, but after a few moments she folded into him as he knew she would. Incredible he had forgotten that…the way she fit with him so perfectly. Incredible he had forgotten the way they'd first met, when he'd arrived at the Corvey Institute, burnt out and exhausted, and she'd been temporarily assigned to his case.

He stroked her hair. "You once told me you wanted to spend the rest of your life with me."

She pulled away from him, but he held on tight.

"You don't remember that?

"No, I never…"

"I do. You know what else I remember? You're grumpy first thing in the morning until you've had your coffee. And you love Christmas but hate New Year's. And your favorite vacation is the time we went to Colorado and made love in a chalet high on the mountaintop."

He tilted her head until he could look into her stunned face. "Audrey Gilbert, you don't remember the first time I told you I love you, but I hope you won't ever forget the second time. I love you, Audrey. I loved you then, and I love you now, and if you think I'm going to let you walk out that door, you're crazier than any hallucination I've ever had."

He didn't wait for a response but crushed his lips against hers, and his heart pounded when she kissed him back. When they moved beyond kissing, he picked her up in his arms and carried her into his bedroom.

And thankfully, there were no hallucinations to distract him.

EPILOGUE

"When did you first know you loved me?" Audrey entwined her fingers with his. They lay among the sheets after reacquainting themselves with each other's bodies. Of course, she couldn't remember the other times they'd made love, only he could. He'd done a thorough job when he'd erased her memories of him. But he'd been careful to preserve any memories she had without him. And his family didn't know about her—his feelings for Audrey had developed so gradually as they had worked on the Ignotus project together, and the threat to her life had happened so quickly, there hadn't been time for introductions.

"The first time or the second time?" he teased.

"How about both times?"

"The first time was the day you took me to meet your mom in the hospital. Chelsea was still a senior in high school, and you had just moved your mom into a new facility and were helping your sister apply for college scholarships. As I watched how you cared for everyone in your life, I remember thinking how lucky I was to have found such an amazing, strong woman to love."

He punctuated each of his words with a kiss.

"I wish I remembered that. And when was the second time?"

"The second time was the day I was sick in the bushes and you held me on the porch."

She giggled. "Seriously? You fell in love with me after throwing up?"

He kissed her pert little nose and each of her individual freckles. "I did. I couldn't wait to see you the next day, remember? I met you at the door."

She wrinkled her nose. "As I recall, you were more excited about my coffee than me."

The statement earned her another kiss—a slow one. "Your coffee was an added benefit."

"I can't believe we fell in love with each other twice." *If only I could remember.* Her voice sounded wistful, and the sadness she felt was so strong, he heard the unspoken thought as if she said it aloud.

"Sweetheart, there is a way you can remember. But it will require me to be in your mind."

She raised herself up on one elbow and made a face. "Nothing you haven't done before."

"What I did before was remove someone else's portal. But we could create one of our own. It would allow us to exchange thoughts at will. I could share my memories with you."

"Hmmm."

"Is that a yes?"

"That's an 'I'll need to think about it.' There's something I still don't understand, though. Why did you create a virtual safe in your mind to store your memories of us?"

He grimaced. "That was out of necessity. Over the years, I had built a catalog in my mind of the paranormal signatures of hackers I encountered. I didn't know how valuable the catalog was until Ignotus got wind of it. They wanted to sell it to a foreign government, who would find and kill those on the list."

"That's horrible."

"Yeah, I feel stupid I didn't know it at the time. Ignotus had hired me to work with you on a project to build a virtual safe that could be opened at will. But what they were really after were the signatures. We hadn't quite perfected the safe process—we could make one, but we couldn't open it. One night, another hacker tried to steal the signatures in my head. I fought him off and learned he was hired by Ignotus. I was worried he'd come after you to get to me. To protect you, I erased your memories of me and built the virtual safe in my mind."

"But why erase your own memories?"

"That wasn't planned. As I said, the process of creating a virtual safe still had a few bugs. In my haste to capture the signatures and lock them away, I accidentally captured my memories of you and more. Afterwards, I didn't know I had a virtual safe in my mind or remember our relationship. That's when Hilda and Abe made their first appearance. I think some part of me knew what I had done and was trying to get my attention."

"I'm so grateful to Hilda and Abe. They brought you back to me."

He leaned forward and kissed her. "I'm grateful, too." He winked. "Now, I'll have free therapy from here on out."

She raised her eyebrows. "Hey, watch it, mister. As I recall, we still have a contract requiring you to pay up for services rendered… Why the sudden serious face?"

He gazed down on the woman he loved and tried to not to worry about her answer. But if Abe and Hilda had taught him anything about himself, it was that all the answers he needed were inside of him.

"What do you say we turn that contract into a marriage license?"

She framed his face with her palms and gazed into his eyes. "Are you asking me to marry you?" *I can't believe this is happening.*

He laughed, but his heart was beating way too fast. "I am. I can't believe you're tormenting me this way."

A slow smile lit up her face like the sun. "Did you just read my mind?" *Read this, my love: Yes, yes, a million times, yes.*

His heart lurched forward, his breathing resumed, and he didn't catch any thoughts after that as he was too busy demonstrating how much he loved her.

OTHER BOOKS BY AMANDA UHL

Mind Waves, Mind Hackers Series, Book 1
Cross Waves, Mind Hackers Series, Book 2
Charmed By Charlie